Julia McKinlay

outskirts
press

Gobelin
All Rights Reserved.
Copyright © 2023 Julia McKinlay
v6.0

This is a work of fiction. Names, characters, businesses, places, events, locales, and incidents are either the products of the author's imagination or used in a fictitious manner. Any resemblance to actual persons, living or dead, or actual events is purely coincidental.

The opinions expressed in this manuscript are solely the opinions of the author and do not represent the opinions or thoughts of the publisher. The author has represented and warranted full ownership and/or legal right to publish all the materials in this book.

This book may not be reproduced, transmitted, or stored in whole or in part by any means, including graphic, electronic, or mechanical without the express written consent of the publisher except in the case of brief quotations embodied in critical articles and reviews.

Outskirts Press, Inc.
http://www.outskirtspress.com

ISBN: 978-1-9772-6166-3

Cover Photo © 2023 Julia Dement. All rights reserved - used with permission.

Outskirts Press and the "OP" logo are trademarks belonging to Outskirts Press, Inc.

PRINTED IN THE UNITED STATES OF AMERICA

Acknowledgment
with
Faith and Gratitude

God
My family for their unending support
Tamera Dryden my friend and editor
Diane Hansen for her friendship and support
Countless storytellers, artists and
historians for their inspiration
Gobelin Tapestry
In this year of our Lord 2023
I say
Thank You

W hat is that? That is something to be used and discarded, as in "ah chew." That is a gift, "hand me that, please." That is the present, the past and the future. That is a way to go; a path into the unknown. That is the surprise unforeseen on the path. That is a beginning, all beginning's begin with a prayer, That is love. That is distance, which is time, which is eternity. I am That, you are That, all this is That, That alone is.*

The island at first sight appeared peaceful, it's warm, wind torn shores deserted. The sea grass and sand melted together in soft tones.. The expansive sky was washed in comforting blue and mirrored the lazy translucent waves that lapped in slow, lazy repetition on the unresponsive shoreline. A tiny boat approached and a young girl peeked over the lip of the bow, inquisitive, but apprehensive. There was no sense of foreboding, no menace lurked in the flat landscape, there was a distinct feeling of loneliness, like forgotten laundry left on the line, becoming stiff and dusty.

Slowly the nutshell of a vessel crawled to the island and beached itself, the waves rocking the girl with a neglectful hand on a baby's cradle. She, being who she was, stepped out of her craft with suspicion, her defensives peaked. Her foot touched the wet dull sand, and something should have changed, a tone in the wind, a peak of interest from the island itself, but nothing, the island went on as it always had, with a decided detachment. Gobelin had, in its own way, welcomed its first inhabitant, a girl by the name of Aage. The promise of Gobelin's magic lay secret and hidden behind the ever present wind and sky.

---

* The Rig Veda (author unknown)

Aage

Aage was born on a cold, windy isle that was rocky and sparse, far north from Gobelin. Her people were fisher folk who kept small herds of sheep and lonely milk cows. Everything they had came from the island, or had been washed ashore in the icy waves. Ships would occasionally anchor and trade with them, parchment and citrus fruit, for wool and cheese. They decorated their homes with weathered whalebone and driftwood, bereft of joy and laughter. They ate seaweed, fish, meat, and milk. The rough grasses that sprouted in the spring were just enough to keep the livestock thin, the women harvested a small store of grain for flat bread. The five families that populated the island were all related, all zealously religious. Their faith held them in a grip of fear, bereft of loveliness or warmth, they stressed sin and damnation. Living constantly in the eye of their neighbor, who looked for any slip, any reason to claim falsehood or repentance. Life was especially hard for the women, but even more so for the children, who were brought into the world to work. There was no play, or proper schooling, scripture was required learning, the only needed learning. And work, there was always work to be done; driftwood and seaweed to gather, fish to clean, livestock to tend, wool to comb and spin, laundry to be washed and mended, food to be cooked; an endless stream of duties that required only hands. Nothing happened which was not necessary. All energy was spent on survival.

Aage had never been beautiful, that was true. She had been weathered and scrawny most of her life. She also had never been hugged, or kissed, caressed, or allowed to disappear under a downy blanket of giggles. There were no ribbons or combs, colorful skirts or soft entrancing scents. The feminine of Aage had been strictly forbidden, as with all the girls of the isle.

Aage soon learned to hold her tongue, born with a sharp wit and controlling nature brought only harsh punishment. The punishments were shared among the families with humiliating public whippings. At an early age she had seen her mother withstand a horrible beating, by her father, in the midst of her neighbors, for a minor infraction. She had left the sheep to graze too long, tending to her brother who had a cough. Aage loved her mother; she was soft and at bed often ended prayers with a smile, a sad smile of hope for the coming morning. It was the becoming of Aage's hardest edge.

Aage slipped into womanhood at fifteen years of age, that horrible sin of being a woman came upon her. Her father had shaken his head in disappointment; "you too have fallen in the grace of God" he had said. Perhaps he thought she had been beyond the sin of womanhood, or hoped so because of her age, but it was his own righteousness that he felt had failed in the eye of God. From that time forward she became someone different in her father's eyes, a testament of his own faith, a sinner, a woman. He ignored her with all his might and watched Aage from a distance. She would fall, and he would be there to snare her deceit.

Aage's father was a bold and abusive man. He held a powerful standing within the small island community, being a faithful servant of God, he often gave sermons on the Sabbath and was one of the five Heads of Family. He sat in judgment against any wrongdoing, or abuse that was brought to the council. He was tall and straight, thin of bone, but strong from his long days fishing and working on the sea. He kept a strong and unrelenting hand on his family, having the word of God to uphold his own reign. But as Aage grew his imagination wandered under her wool garments, he wondered what was happening under there, and what she looked like without them. He took this imagining as bewitchment, praying and repenting in his private prayers. He asked God what restraint was required of such a man as himself, a man who had trusted and believed, upheld the voice of God in his home? His own vanity answered with justification, he had every right to know. He was her father, whom but himself should witness the abomination of sin, and know it without a fault. Whom but himself could curb its destructive course?

It had been half-a-year since Aage had noticed her father's stare. She had kept her knowing silent, but defensive. The women of the island did not always keep their tongues in the manner that their men folk instructed, and she had a growing distrust of her father's keen gaze. Her father's eye had always been diligent and made Aage feel helplessly small when she had been a child, but this new interest left her feeling vulnerable and afraid. Aage felt as if she were about to be struck with his wide flat palm. It transcended religious belief, tradition, parenthood, she knew he was looking at her as a man looks at a woman. Her **Father**! Soon after she realized his intent Aage knew that she could not stay on the island. Her heart told her so, she was destined to go beyond its rocky coast, and she prepared.

    Aage began stealing things and hiding them away. She took clothes from the mending basket, dried salted fish, a sheep bladder, and a small box made of wood that kept secret treasures. She felt the time was growing close, she could feel her father's pent up agitation building, to what could only be a painful conclusion. Her mother had a wide-eyed look of confusion and helplessness, these passing day's were hurtful for her, but she never matched her husband's behavior to Aage, and Aage kept her fears to herself.
    It was the height of summer on the island, a time of hard labor to harvest the island of its sparse gifts and enjoy the warm days. Aage's father commanded the family to stay inside their house, giving them insignificant tasks in a brusque, unquestionable insistence. He left the house and went to the far side of the township, surveying its secretive nooks. He knew the island like his own prayer book; he was searching for something in a context he had never looked before. He spent the day scrabbling in the rocks; searching the coastline, he had known since childhood, fettering out its secret places, judging it's compliance. He returned at sunset, sweaty and

disheveled, in bad temper and demanding dinner. That evening's prayers were particularly intense, entirely focused on the child's duty to obey their parent. That night in his own bed he surprised his wife with uncensored attention delivered without kindness.

    The next day, after her father's strange behavior, Aage stole her most precious item. A boat, a child's boat. It was an impish little wooden structure, looking more like a nutshell than a boat. It had no stern or sail, only a small paddle, and was large enough for her to curl up in the bottom. Made from driftwood and a cowhide, slick with tallow, the little boat could travel far from shore, but dubious if it could return. Aage hid the small vessel under a rocky cliff that was difficult to get to and out of sight, but uncomfortably close to the township. She packed it with her small store of goods and covered it with an old fishing net too damaged to mend.

    Aage had no idea of where she would go, occasionally boats would come to the island, but very rarely, and she had not been allowed around the men when they were ashore. They always arrived out of the south during the warmer months, but never stayed, they were discouraged to stay ashore by the island's men folk. If they had news of other lands, it was kept from the women and children. But, Aage thought, if they could make it to this island, other land must not be far off. Aage decided she would head south, the wind was smooth from the west and the current could carry her south, surely there would be something.

    Aage waited, the waning summer was inviting and secure, the season seemed to have a calming effect on everyone, a gentle adherence to what is comfortable and familiar. Aage's father became content, settled in his own skin and seemed to savor the time he spent on the ocean, coming home tired and complete. Aage began to think of her pending departure as a daydream, to explore other places and meet friendly faces, much like a child who builds a secret fort and becomes for a moment the worldly pirate, with all the exotic mysticism of the unknown surrounding the imagination. Maybe her father would rescind his message and become her father again. It was what she wished and prayed for; perhaps she could please him as a daughter, and not leave the home.

The short summer drew to its close; soon the autumn celebrations would begin. The sky would cloud with whispers of red, scarfed around the setting sun. The smooth sea would work itself into roaring waves that would attempt to take refuge on the pebble sand. It was time to gather all the driftwood from the shore and round the sheep into their winter pens. The wind shifted from the north, bringing a chill, that swirled with the warm winds from the west. Aage found herself caught in these same winds, longing for the comfort of the island's tradition, her dream of leaving almost forgotten as a childish summer infatuation.

The first day of autumn came as a quiet breath from a sleeping child. Aage hung the freshly washed linen sheets out on the line to dry, against the palette of a hazy yellow sky, the sun muffled in a high foggy embrace. She relaxed with a long slow sigh. Summer seemed a long ago dream, she would stay here with her family. Perhaps she would marry. Her mother's cousin had a boy, he had stood at procession all summer, and looked intently at her as he showed Aage's family to their positions. He had the same look as all the islanders, a bit rocky and rough hewn, but with his own tender way about him. There was room for a small cottage, in their families compound, back from the rest, with it's own bit of rough pasture and sheltered from the sea. They could have a good life there to start, maybe even a child or two, after a bit. Aage was staring without seeing, the linen hanging limp in her hand dragging in the brown dust, she was lost under a warm blanket of future dreams. A small movement, a shadow playing on the ground almost caught her attention, Aage did not see the wide flat palm of her father until it was upon her. She turned in time to take his slap full across her check.

The morning shattered as Aage landed at her father's feet. He was shouting at her, she knew he was, but the words were drowned in the ringing of her ears. She had let her guard down. That must be what he was shouting about. She had forgotten, had become comfortable, had stepped back into her place in the family, Aage had not even realized that she had been removed until that moment. Aage tried to stand, but her father's hands were on her shoulders picking her up and tossing her like he would toss a caught fish. Her face was smashed into the dirt, her father was still yelling, mumbling disjointed words, using the voice of sermon, something about teaching the devil. He held her head into the dirt, and her dress was being raised, dull fumbling between her legs and then he entered her. Aage felt the huge weight of his body crushing her, and she thought, "is this it?" and then she felt the pain ripping through her and she cried out. He was saying, "You are not my daughter, You are not my daughter," over and over. And then he was done. He stood over her and said "you are a witch, you bewitched me, and the devil himself has taken over you." And he was gone. Aage did something she would never do again, she fainted.

The air was dark with gray clouds when Aage returned to the dirt in her face. Her arms were weak, her legs shaking; she could still feel the invasion as a dark pounding shame between her legs. Voices were questioning around her; her ears picked up the nuance of anger, the soft voice of her mother in striking defense. And once again she was being handled, picked up onto her melting legs that would not meet, on to her feet, that would not work. Dirt was lodged in her mouth, she coughed and spit. Rough hands moved her, harsh words surrounded her, and Aage vomited.

She was dragged by her arms, many people were around her, but she could not see, life was a blur of pain. Her mother was close by, she knew it and called out to her, she listened for comfort through the ringing darkness. Her father's presence was absent. She was struck by something hard on her back and stumbled, her arms were ripped upward and she was dragged along. The voices were louder now, many had joined, and a chorus of "WITCH, WITCH" was being chanted. She was on the beach now and could look up, the entire community was at the shore, the women stood behind the men, the men of the island surrounded Aage.

The trial began, the trial of a witch. The headmen of the council faced Aage, all held the book of God open and began to read. She knew every word, condemnation, and punishment. She thought this could not be, and she cried tears, hot and pitiful. Her father had given his statements. After the rape of Aage he had gone to the council and denounced his own daughter as a witch. Aage was sentenced to banishment.

The autumn day was closing; the sun covered in a gray cloth of cloud as it met the horizon. Aage looked for her mother, who stood clutching her throat in pain. Aage broke the circle, and tried to run to her. The men stopped her and threw her against the sand. "GO WITCH, GO WITCH". Stones hit Aage and she was driven to the water. The boy she had dreamed of beginning a life with stood with his head proud as he raised his arm. Her mother turned away and Aage saw her father standing behind the crowd with righteous arrogance allowing the council to do his work for him. Aage was forced into the sea.

The cold seawater penetrated her clothes and the waves pushed her back to the shore. Her people standing against her escape continued to throw stones. Aage called to her mother, crying, her body an enemy to her survival had none of its strength. Finally the sea took her, and she was floating beyond salvation in its salty embrace.

This was the moment Aage would always remember, the whole of her life standing in defiance of her existence. The waves curled around her, carrying her from the shore, the cold seeping into her bones, her family turning away, when the miracle happened. The sun dipped into the sea and the fog ran to her cries. The shore, with its host of hostility became enveloped in gray, and so did Aage.

Aage became invisible. She swam, not to the shore, but took its parallel path to her summer dream. Her boat and store of goods were close. She could still hear voices from the beach, as she made her way to the tiny boat. Aage, the damned, stripped the boat of its netting, took off her wet clothing and left it on the shore, replacing it with the stored clothes she had so knowingly stowed away. They were not completely dry, but better than she had. Aage spent little time recovering; she launched her little vessel and relinquished her life into the arms of the sea, paddling away from her island home in the growing darkness. Finally she curled into a ball at the bottom of the boat and did not care where the sea took her, or if she would be among people again, or if she would ever wake up.

Aage washed ashore on the deserted island of Gobelin, how long she was adrift she did not know. The island welcomed her with a warm breeze, filled with the scent of sweet flowers. There was cool spring water and long grasses that hissed with movement. Autumn never touched this island; it lived in perpetual spring and summer. The transparent blues of the shallow waters were calm and inviting. Aage ate the flowers; their colorful sprays across the island were so sweet and charming she wanted to become part of them. This gift would last her entire life. That the island was lonely of people pleased Aage beyond relief. She scoured its shore and hiked its hills, and made a home in the western corner, where the warmest winds settled and could be still. The coast of this corner of the island was surrounded by cliffs, with only a stiff stair of rock leading to Aage's hideaway. No one could take her by surprise if they approached by sea; her home was a lookout over the entire island. Aage didn't consider herself shipwrecked, she had come home, and she claimed the island as her own.

It was an accident when Aage found honey. She had lived on the fish that crawled out of the sea, the flowers that gave themselves so willingly and eggs from the birds that nested in the cliffs. She scavenged daily. During an adventurous expedition she heard bees humming. She watched them with suspicion, taking pollen from her flowers and gathering in a paper nest. They swooped and buzzed in their busy task, and she wondered what they did there. She took to spending her days observing them, when without warning the weight of the bee hive exceeded it's anchor and the nest fell. The agitated bees swarmed to save their home while the honey glistened from it's broken shell. The bees were in fierce commotion and their attention focused when Aage waved them away and took the honey. She took it to her small shelter and tasted sweetness for the first time. A true sweetness, that was unlike the milk from a cow or goat. This was the beginning of the obsession that would create her life.

Aage was as happy as circumstance allowed her to be. Her family she thought of frequently in the first months, with mixed emotions of desired acceptance, and anxious fear that she would be found. It was not long before she cast aside religious expectation. No one demanded it of her, and the warmth of the island soothed any compensation it may have required. Her prayers were short and internal, "please let me find food today." In a moment of doubt, "Are you here?", she would ask. With the discovery of honey this latter question was answered and Aage did not again question the existence of God, or his presence in her life. Ritual was unnecessary, survival was, and it was her work.

Aage knew she was pregnant, her growing belly told her so. At first she thought the "curse of women" had left her because she no longer lived among men, but the truth was soon apparent. She gave birth to a boy, at the shore allowing the waves to wash over her, their strength pushing and pulling, easing the pain. When the face appeared between her legs she grasped hold and yanked, looking to see if it were a girl, as she hoped. She planned to keep a girl, but a boy she would let go and allow the waves to take him. As she held him he was calm and content, as if being born was a soothing massage, his open eyes looking right at her with a knowing stare. She took him back to her shelter.

Aage could not say that she loved the boy, she cared for him. Cared for his needs, fed him, cleaned him, and gave him shelter. She watched him with minute suspicion, wondering if he would "turn", as she thought of it. She pondered all the names that she knew and all brought memories of people she would not bestow on the boy, or herself. She called him Boy. During his youngest years she often wished she had let the sea take him, he was demanding and required all of her attention. As he approached the age of five, she set him to doing chores. Gathering eggs and flowers, but he often lost attention and would run from her, laughing in a carefree manner that she had never seen before. This was the one aspect of Boy that befuddled Aage, he laughed. He laughed when the sun came up, or went down, when the wind tickled his neck or the stars came out. Boy was amazed at life; he spent hours examining the flowers, turning over stones to see what lived beneath them, the butterflies he would play gently with, and the fish he chased in the shallows. He gave an eye to anything new and relished its existence. He would often leave and not return in the same day to their growing home, which angered Aage. He called her Aage. He seemed to be young and old, oblivious to the insecurity of Aage's structured experience.

Together they constructed the gardens. Boy's unlimited imagination was the crux of their complexity. He would dream of a garden, and begin its evolution; Aage followed along, nay saying his vision, but at its completion relenting with "yes this is what I want", neither giving credit nor acknowledgment to the other. Boy hummed while he worked, tunes that had no meaning or explanation, and this manner was strange to Aage. Boy made himself a drum from a hollow driftwood log, and infuriated Aage with his nonsensical pounding that to him were full of structure. Aage's son was beyond her comprehension; her short experience would not allow her the luxury of his carefree nature. They argued about the order of things, "you cannot do that!" "Why not"? He would counter. Aage had not left her upbringing; Boy never saw its value.

Boy could make friends with the birds, that almost magically had appeared on the island when Aage had touched its shores. He collected their spent feathers and brought them to Aage. "What are these for?" She complained, Boy with his sweet smile ignored the complaint and held them at her waist, "They could be a skirt. I can help." He spoke tenderly. Aage's clothing had slowly been hacked into coverings for Boy. Together they fashioned Aage a small wardrobe. One day she could be an exotic queen from a foreign land with a train of peacock glory, or a young bride in white sprayed with wildflowers. Aage never did say thank you, Boy didn't look for acknowledgment, he could see, she walked different.

Boy made pigments from the flowers and stones, and colored the wax made by the bees. He strung candles about their home like wind chimes for their voices. The honey he left to Aage, who grumbled about the difficult task, she must undertake all on her own. She stored the honey away in the waxy vials seasoned with herbs and flowers that Boy created for her. The gardens were complete when Boy reached the age of fifteen. They rayed around their small dwelling as a living sundial of beauty, humming to the flow of the island.

Their lives mingled in this ponderous way, through Boy's light heart and Aage' established mistrust. Constantly pushing and pulling at each other with growing distance. Boy was tall and strong, becoming a man, with his father's face and his grandmother's secret kindness. Boy left the island without any forethought. He had reached the age of seventeen, his youth and playful nature reaching an apex of maturity that pulled him to thoughts beyond the island. He had never known anyone but Aage, and this seemed unnatural to him. She was unnatural to him. He stood one day on the beach of Gobelin and dove into the crystal waves, their warmth urged him on, go deeper, go farther, the voice entrancing and sweet. A ship, full of men, picked him up, not a league from the shore of Gobelin, which they never did see. They did not understand a word of what he said, but accepted him as a token of good luck that they would find strong, bountiful catch. Boy traveled south with them and soon forgot Aage, until years later he would need her.

Aage had no idea of where Boy had got to. She thought for a while that he was hiding from her and she roamed the island calling his name. But after a season had passed without him she gave up looking. Often she burst out in speech "where are you Boy?" she would say while hunting eggs, or gathering seaweed. She would not admit that she missed him, "trouble and inconvenience was all he amounted too". "Only one mouth to feed and the work of twenty to be done", she would mumble.

Aage grew more and more disheveled and angry, while the gardens matured and settled. She tended the honey, making her own wax vials "better'n his" she would shout out loud. It took nine years, two months and twenty-two days to burn all of the candles that Boy had created. The house was numb with his absence on that day for Aage, the day he truly left. There was nothing left of Boy on the island, the drum had long ago washed away, his laughter long ago had stopped haunting her days. She cried that day, the first time since she had cried for her mother at the shore while the men threw stones at her. She thought of the boy she had dreamed of a life with and her heart was empty. Aage felt that life had abandoned her at the beginning of its heartbeat.

What Aage did not know is that the day that Boy left her, a thousand miles from Gobelin, Ioman was born.

Ioman

The savannah swelled with yellow green grasses that shimmer in African heat. Low slung trees stretch above the land with the grace of a mother bending to pick up a crying child. Blue sky reached beyond the horizon, holding flat shreds of cloud in their voyage above the earth. The gazelle slept peacefully in the shadows, comforted by years of living closely with the people who call themselves The Azures.

There are dangers here that lurk in the soft shadows, a lazy almost sleepy danger that naps in the heat. Lions roam the land, and the great elephant, wild boar keep their own vigilant, fierce homes, not unlike the humans who shared the land. The unconsciously gentle giraffe with their wild swaying necks. Snakes swim through the grass with grace and delicate caution. The Azures live in perfect complex composure with this array of life, they mirror the wild community within their own family structures.

The Azures are a dark and exotic tribe. The people are full and tall, with bright round faces and broad smiles, flat noses and softly arching brows over almond shaped eyes, always of the deepest, dark night sky. The women's bodies are pear shaped, with round inviting bottoms and bowl shaped bellies under smallish, pointing breasts. The men are equal in their own beauty, with full shoulders and strong tall legs. The women grow their hair long, a sign of health and prosperity, that is braided into long snakes adorned with beads. The men keep their heads shaved, a sign of strength and fearlessness.

Life is far from lazy here on the flat grassland, that is a day march to the sea. Although the heat slows things to a standstill, the Azures are never still; even when sitting they are aware and cautious, watching. Time clicks as methodically as the pestle against grain. The Azures are a matriarchal society, the childbearing women having hold on all tribal decisions. Children live with their mothers, a female child will live with their mother until they gather their own hut, at around the age of fifteen, but the male children are sent out to live in the savannah at puberty, until a woman takes them in. A woman may take as many husbands as she wishes, and men may have as many wives. The home always belongs to the woman, if she accepts a husband, her present man must leave and go back to the savannah. As a man grows old he would find himself on the doorstep of the woman who bore his first child. His children would care for him, and his wife, even if she shared her home with another, he would be accepted on her porch.

Ioman's mother had five children, four girl children and Ioman, the last. He bathed in their attention from infancy. His sisters often teasing that they would dress him as a girl and keep him forever with them. They floated him in their love, giving him the best food and drink, fanning him in the heat and praising him as a great hunter, when he brought home a small hare or snake. If he cried they cuddled around him till he grinned in satisfaction, if he grew angry they submitted to his whim and catered to his desire. Ioman was comfortably spoiled by his own harem of women, and declared that he would not leave and go to the savannah with his father. It was a silent mother that heard his words, his time to leave was less than a year away, and she would have no second thought about sending him out of the home to make him into a man.

The time passed slowly. Things were changing for the Azures; rumbles from the Lassana tribe to the east were becoming more frequent. They wanted the clear path to the sea and the Azures stood in the way. The land was sculpted by a great shallow river that wound it's way through a high canyon, the eastern tribe had to traverse hard land to get to the sea, the easy path was directly through the Azures land. There had always been skirmishes between the two neighbors, but the violence was increasing. Six men died in the tall grass, good strong men, ambushed by scouts; one morning the women awoke to find all of the chickens dead in their pens, not from snakes or wild scavengers, brutally mutilated as a message and the war began.

The weakness of the Azures lifestyle was plain to their enemies. The women were unprotected and untrained in defense. Most lived in transition, with children; their men were waiting for their women's motion of acceptance. They were unsuspecting of violence. The men were hunters, unprepared to be hunted by other men, many were slaughtered in the first attack. The Azures first line of defense weakened in the assault. Their enemy attacked at night, surrounding the men in the grass silently, they lit torches timed by the moon set. Their bodies painted in hideous colors of blood red and white, their hair tangled with the feathers of birds, long spears in their hands, that were strong and wicked in the dark. The enemy shouted loud insults and war cries and overtook the men of the Azures quickly. Ioman's father survived the attack and alerted the women and men in the village.

Ioman remembered him at this moment; he would not stand on his wife's porch, even in time of terror, he stood outside and called to him. His first son, who long ago he had left. He called to him, Ioman, now fourteen, to take up a weapon and join him. Ioman trembled, not wanting to leave his family, but he went. Together they woke the Azures and made a heroic stand at the mouth of the river that the Azures controlled. It was a bloody battle, many of Ioman's people died, many children were left motherless, many of the men were killed, and they were defeated. The Azures fled to the south, and left the mouth of the river open to their enemies.

Two of Ioman's sisters were killed or taken by the enemy, his mother was stabbed through the heart by a spear twice her height, as she defended her children. Ioman's father was killed at the heart of the battle, in the center of the river, fighting hand to hand with the chieftain of the enemy. They took each other's lives.

The Azures lives changed, their village overtaken. They were tormented and ridiculed by their oppressors who would not be consoled with right of passage to the sea, they would kidnap and kill the Azures at whim, cocky with dominance, they would only be satisfied with the overtaking of the Azures completely.

Ioman was now sixteen, an orphan, and the sole supporter of his two remaining sisters. He was angry, he was a man full of resolve. He stood over six feet, and weighed close to a full water buffalo. His arms could swallow three snakes, his legs were as strong as the river flow. He was as black as a night without a moon, while his smile held the sun. He told his sisters that it would end, their lives would no longer be subject to another's.

Ioman commanded the assault on the enemy. Every man or boy child was equipped with a weapon. Under a dark sky they stole north up the river to the Azures village, now home of their enemy. The Lassana had kept the village to the east and could control a long stretch of the river.

Under Ioman's order they silently killed every person they found, woman, child or man. No prisoners were taken, no beg was heeded. Ioman's youngest sister was found during the raid and brought home. The Azure men waited outside of the enemy camp, hidden by brush and grass, anticipating their response to the violent attack. Ioman harbored a deep resentment after the killing of his parents. He was driven with hatred.

On a moonless night the enemy moved, the Azure men waited for them. They had dug graves for their enemies and covered them with grass mats, lying on the ground with spears ready, the trap was set. They watched as the scouts came and went, and saw when the news of their peoples violent end arrived; they watched as anger boiled over, mixed with pain and injustice. The Azures watched them council, prepare and move from their camp, from the abandoned homes of the Azures. Ioman called each movement of his men, his success as leader of the tribe unquestioned, even by the women, forever changing the structure of the Azures, a man would lead them. He held a confidence that was unshakable, a gentle nature that would not be mistaken for vulnerability. His presence was warm and inviting, with a caution of truth, no lie could pass through him undetected. The pampered boy was gone, he stood a man who would not surrender, would allow no frivolous proposition. If Ioman laughed, everyone laughed; if he were stoic, all were stoic. Every man stood behind each word he spoke, he lead them into battle and they would die for him.

The enemy moved, driven by emotion, their weakness, Ioman surmised. The Azures were waiting for them. Motionless they waited as the enemy approached, they had spread out, just as Ioman strategize, marching four to five feet apart, like searchers for something lost. If they had come in single file Ioman's plan would have been thwarted. The African plain demanded the blanket approach, wildlife still posed a threat, snakes in particular, in this way one long line of men would not be visible, they could easily form a circle around the Azures, fanning out in both directions.

They were caught in the trap. Ioman's ambush was unanticipate. The enemy fell as one into the hidden pits the Azures had dug for them and died beneath waiting spears. The pit was lit on fire, a warning to any whom had stayed behind. Few escaped and those that did vanished into the savannah, the Azures moved back into their homes.

Two years had passed since Ioman saw his father and mother die, the river was theirs again and Ioman went home to live again with his sisters.

The Azures settled back into life, celebration and mourning blended into their daily ritual with an acute awareness of the unknown. The family homes were overflowing with children and women and displaced men come home. Some of the men went back to the savannah, with new watchfulness; they were comfortable on the plain. With instruction from Ioman the men slept in shifts. They could no longer ponder the sweetness of being attached to a woman. The river with its round curves and graceful lines still posed a threat to the Azures. No one had approached them, their reputation had spread far along the coast and through the interior of the land as vicious and vengeful, the peaceful Azures no longer existed in the minds of neighboring tribes.

Ioman could not sit still in his sister's home. Soon he joined the men on the savannah. Ioman stayed on the savannah for a year, many women offered their home to him, he was the warrior, but he took none of their advances and kept his gaze vigilantly outward. He was satisfied with the time he spent with the other men, but felt an empty spot where he would have sat with his own father.

Ioman made an unprecedented decision, he would build his own home. The graceful curve of the river lined with its polished stones gave him a feeling of contentment and peace. He used the stones for the walls of his home. The other men became distracted by his enthusiasm. His idea was to build a secret structure that would blend into the river and embrace the steep bank, concealed within the natural landscape, providing him a natural guard stand. The roof of Ioman's house became pockets of staircases that allowed the entrance of a single man to a strategic lookout.

Three years passed for the Azures, the society fell into a power struggle. The women wanted to go back to the old ways, but the men knew the women couldn't control the river without them. The men were now an army. They would marry, but it was his decision to leave her home. The men no longer thought of women in a long term, they were occupied with military vigilance. The soft willing body of the woman did not commit their attention. A child born to a woman could have been any man's, and the boy children could not wait to leave their mother's homes. The tribe fell into disarray.

Ioman had no children. He would visit the women's huts, but would stay for one night only. The mothers willingly offered their daughters to the great warrior in the hopes of gaining status by bearing him a child. Ioman was not taken by any of the girls, he relished the thought of a woman, one woman who could stand beside him and be his equal; he wanted a queen. He wanted no children by the old measures of the Azures. A woman who would join him in his own house. On the occasion that he would visit the women's village he looked for the one, and found all the women tired, subservient, lacking in pride, but flush with arrogance and unnatural coyness.

He was pondering this predicament when Searlait took a bath on his doorstep.

Searlait

Searlait haled from a nomadic tribe that traveled the great Arid Desert, who called themselves Gens D'Etoile. They were traders of blankets and jewelry. They traveled east to west during the winter solstice, following the sun, and traveled back on an elliptical circle at the celebration of the summer solstice. The Great River they crossed twice each year at the equinoxes, and its smaller tributaries at their counterparts. They moved farther south in the cooler months and farther north in the warmer months. They varied little with whom they traded, mysterious and secretive in their business, they kept to themselves, and were silent and stoic in demeanor when they met "de la Terre", as they called everyone who was not them.

All the women of the Gens D'Etoile originated from one perfect woman. Their bodies were sinewy, small of bone with soft undulating curves. Their hips were small and light. Their breasts, handful's of taut flesh that airily kept watch on the sky. Small soft curls of dark hair covered their round noble heads. Fine boned noses and high check bones accentuated large eyes, the color of sunrise on sand, over voluptuous tender tinted lips. Their skin conjured a recipe of rose petals drizzled with honey. Centuries of inter marriage had polished these women, every common gene had been weeded out, every unfortunate mannerism left neglected by evolution. The result was a woman of gracious, noble beauty and a childlike manner, who was easy to smile.

The men were not so endowed; they had the same stature, but managed to look scrawny. Large knees and elbows, the fine features were pinched, and instead of the fine smooth brow they had a bushy protruding shelf. Their skin was shadowy and uneven, with a whitish cast. The only beauty they shared with their life companions was a large, sweetly endearing, often seen smile.

In the privacy of their camps they walked naked, the women wearing only dark indigo blue veils about their heads, weighted with silver chain. They adorned themselves with silver jewelry, all crafted in circles, with tiny charms of astral remembrances. They wore simple sandals of woven camel hair. They were a mischievous and playful people.

All of the movements and secrets of the Gens D'Etoile were based on a very simple belief. They had been cast like die onto the desert bed by the great star God, the Sun.

At one time they had all been stars, placed carefully among the other stars. Part of the timeless eternity, the scope of their contribution yet to be discovered. They claim to have petitioned the Sun with their purpose in the cool darkness, but had received The Sun's patient patter, "All things reveal themselves in Time". So they followed the metronome of the Sun God for what seemed ages upon ages, the Gens D'Etoile became restless. They would fall to amuse themselves, or visit with other stars and so would be missed in the perfection of the starry plan. And one most adventurous star while sailing the universe fell in love. This star refused to return to his appointed star place, and would not abandon this new falling. He and his love, the blue star of Delaisser, hid from God. The Sun God became very angry, frustrated with this lot of truant children they were expelled from the open darkness of their spacey home to the white heat of the desert, to the star that was not a star. Under his watchful eye they traveled restlessly over the hot sand. Orbiting, as they should have done long ago. The wide open night sky a reminder of their true home, their rightful place in the universe, a glaring hole for all to see. Their restless nature was to blame for their heavenly dismissal, and they hoped that one day the Sun God would lift them from the dry white prison and place them gently in their cool, prospective hollows, to twinkle in subdued obedience.

Most of the Gens D'Etoile claimed to be missing from constellations, young boys often claimed to be a penis or head. The boasting calmed with maturity, but at the age of twelve, during a much-anticipated celebration, the boys were told which constellation they belonged and it was tattooed on their body. The girls became a part of their husband's constellation when they married, just in case the Sun God rescinded his sentence. Their star was tattooed on one side, or the other of his own star, perhaps beneath, never above. But it was rare that they didn't treat each other with respect, or love each other, or think the same, or just go along.

When Searlait, warm and moist, entered existence she

was who she would always be. She looked with import at her prospective parents, sized them from head to toe with instinctual knowledge, and accepted them with an imperceptible nod. They weren't great, but they would do. With all the arrogance that only the uninformed can carry off, she behaved as though she had always had the option of choice.

Searlait grew to be as beautiful as her mother, her sisters, cousins, and aunts. She chose to be something else, to be different. While the others wore their blue veils about their heads, she wrapped herself entirely, from her perfectly round head to her scrubbed pink toes. She rarely showed her face, and then only to her immediate family. Layers of blue veil concealed her movement and form. She hid beneath them, a perpetual game of hide and seek, with no seeker. The tribal leaders questioned her parents, had something happened to her? Was she no longer beautiful? Modesty was not known by any of them, but this is what her mother attributed to the awkward behavior, promising that it would pass as she grew into womanhood. Grudgingly the tribe acquiesced, still suspicious, but what harm could it bring? She would eventually lose the strange inhibition that captured her and become one with them.

But like most uncomfortable issues this did not evaporate. Searlait continued her reclusive behavior, and when it came time for her to marry, no one came forward to ask for her. She was available to all the men of the tribe, with the exclusion of her immediate family. It was the custom that young girls be married at the age of fourteen. The men would offer gifts to her parents, rugs, camels, jewelry; the same articles they traded with other tribes on their nomadic trek, hardly anything unusual. Volume was the key to success when it came to acquiring a wife. All of the young girls had numerous suitors, vying at their parents tent doors with offers of riches that had been planned and saved for most of their lives.

No man outside the Gens D'Etoile had ever seen a Gens D'Etoile woman, and no man had ever seen Searlait. Under the veils of modesty that Searlait employed lay the dream she would not dare to share with anyone, not even her mother. Searlait had fashioned a vision in her young heart. She had seen the most perfect man, he was large and very dark, and held in his eyes a kindness for her that she had never known. Searlait did not want the men of the Gens D'Etoile. She had seen a gift, perhaps from the Star God himself, of a path beyond her imagination, beyond the toils of the tribe. She could be patient, and she would cover her beauty to keep the men away from her door and her future.

Searlait did not anticipate that her father could not be so patient. He saw riches that could be his going elsewhere, and a daughter that still needed to be fed and housed. Only his wife could restrain his ranting, she consoled him with sweet words and graceful caresses. Extracting a promise that Searlait could remain with them for a while longer, things would change, she told him. Searlait's mother gave her a basket and told her to go into the desert and collect bees. She filled more than one basket with the tiny demons and learned a great deal about how to sooth their temperament. And when the patience of Searlait's father expired in a fit of violent fury, Searlait took her baskets and camped outside of the tribe's warmth and security. She lived frugally, trading with the women for the things she needed. She traded the sweet golden honey and beeswax that until now had been an unexpected treat to find in the desert. Within the year she became a valuable asset to the tribe, although none but the women ever spoke to her, and she became Dame Meil, the strange one.

Within the tribe every one hundred years marked a new beginning, a herald of new thoughts, strength of what is young and chalk marked the passage of their time on earth. Four hundred of hundred-year passages had elapsed in their memories, from the punishment that brought them to the strange earth. Each century brings a new power and vigor to the tribe. Searlait turned eighteen in the age of Revelation.

For Searlait the truths she needed to face were crusty with the layers of her own inner turmoil. Loneliness emptied her days, pride had stepped over the invisible line of turning back, and acceptance was a blurry shape she had never seen clearly. Her veils were no longer a choice, but a reflection of her heart, shrouded, dark, and secretive. She no longer knew what she looked like. When she looked at her family and tribal sisters, she did not connect with these echoes of herself, who walked freely, with pride in their bodies and faces. She envied them their fullness, their beauty. She would watch them from the darkness and wonder where she was and when she would be found.

On the third morning of the New Year, Searlait went into the desert to gather whatever she could find. Bones, twigs, plants, the harvest of a wasteland. She took a basket of bees with her, young bees without a mother, a comb of honey, a parcel of cheese wrapped in palm leaves and a skin of water. The cool, matronly moon was full, and shone the desert with blue stillness. Shifting winds herded the sand, but it was all the same, stone lined courtyards of sand, dusty pools shaded by rocky umbrellas, and sweet flowers tucked between poignant thorns. She gathered a few precious gifts that day, the bleached skull of a goat, the discarded skin of a snake, bark shards of a date palm, she striped a palm frond of its sinew, and collected three bees for the new hive. She thanked the desert for each gift.

She gathered during the twilight of dawn until the sun greeted her, his crescent arched into an angry welt across the horizon. She knelt to him and wished him, "fair day", and sang gently with her hands cupped to her lips to carry the prayer. The Sun God flared in waves of harsh undulating heat, piercing her with his silently questioning eye. She stood staring in disbelief at her parent, the one who gives and takes away, cast out and enfolds, rewards and punishes. Still breaking the horizon, Searlait was not fully affronted with the Sun's wrath, but she knew it was coming. She had finally come to trial for her aberration. He asked why, and she had no answer, nothing but a child's dream half forgotten, with only the choices of its diversion standing alone and unanchored. He rode into the sky free from the gravity of the horizon, glaring red. Finding herself alone in the desert with the unforgiving God, she ran from him. She could feel his stare on her back, his demanding question as a force pulling her backward. She fell off the edge of a sand shelf into dune shadow and rolled into its canyon. Gathering up her scattered gifts she hid, keeping her head low, hesitantly watching the sky for the suns penetrating rays. She would have to turn east to make her way back to the tribe, but she could calm her heart and perhaps the eye of the Sun would be drawn to other things, and time would calm his temper.

This is how the wind found her, crouching in one of its own canyons. And it whispered secrets, softly caressing with warm tongues of air, Searlait ignored him and crawled along the shadow line. Every member of the Gens D'Etoile knew the character of the wind, it did not like to be ignored, but Searlait was scared and tired, she waved the wind off and spoke aloud, "Adieu, I go now, we will visit another day." The Wind caught his breath, inhaling deeply. She did not confide in the wind and had always thought him untrustworthy and self serving. Searlait felt suddenly caught between two great powers. She tried to run and the soft sand grabbed at her feet and took her sandals. At that moment the wind exhaled at her small retreating back. Following after her, harassing, shamelessly whistling in her ears, whipping her veils, and cutting off her progress with explosions of sand. The seduction forgotten, the wind flowed easily into his true nature. Searlait tried to appease the wind, but He was no longer listening, was dryly attempting to enter her, through her mouth, nose, eyes, vagina. Viciously tried to strip off her veils, but they held their dignity. Out of instinct she struggled, but she knew despite its angry display, if she submitted the wind would lead her to a haven. Surrendering, she was carried above the sand and thrown against a wall of rock that she could shelter against.

Searlait curled into a ball hugging the rock. She put her back to the gusts of sand and tried to tuck her things in front of her. The rock was broken and rent; she struggled to move some of the loose rock in the wall to the front of her in a desperate attempt to block the elements. When her hand suddenly went through the wall and for a moment touched on stillness. She tore at the rock and in a few moments there was an opening she could slip through. She tossed her basket and her gathered treasures in the hole and squeezed her head and torso through as far as she could. She patted the darkness for something solid. Searlait could not hear how far her things had fallen, the wind had been screaming in protest at her escape. She could feel the Sun beating her through the wind, she struggled, feeling her hips wedge in the small opening. With a desperate strain she jerked, just enough to collapse the rock wall and send her to the floor of the cave. She landed in a pool of soft sand with a cascade of broken rock falling about her.

Searlait lay quiet, searching in her mind for pain, tracing her body like a map. She decided she was not hurt badly, bruised from the falling rock, mostly on her legs. She sat up and searched gingerly for her things. They were not far from her, she could hear the bees in loud complaint and using a now accentuated sense of touch she identified the desert's treasures. The basket of bees had not lost its lid, which was strapped to itself, but Searlait made sure none could escape, carefully examining the lid's small circumference. She could see the movement of the wind's shadow through the cave opening, with the little light that penetrated into the darkness of the cave. Searlait untied the knot at her neck that held her veil about her head. She removed her face veil and tied them both around the basket. The air tasted cool and old, and instantly Searlait's senses rose in upright attention, her nose strained to leave her face, each cell in her body repeated the single life giving word, water. There was water in this unexpected refuge.

Sweet water, not spoiled, not acrid with mineral; the kind of water that drips deliciously from a parched tongue. Searlait moved with instinct. The west wall tapered south, leaving a narrow strip of sand till the rock walls met. She was glad of the dark, her sense of smell heightened, she smelled the rock like an animal, not hurried, deliberate. Touching the stone gently for crevasses. The water was on the other side of this rock. The wall was different from the rock that had cascaded away from her touch; no amount of shoving would move this. This was a dead end, but cool sweetness filled her nostrils like the scent of a lover. Now she needed light.

She surveyed her store of goods, she could make light. She tied the sinew of palm around her big toes and balanced the shard of wood between them in the goat skull. She placed her hands firmly behind her and used the strength in her legs to twist the contraption in quick repetition.

She could smell the skull heating and carefully placed the snakeskin, it caught. The smell was acrid, oily, but a flame sprang into life. She squeezed the honey from its comb and smoothed the wax around the palm sinew.

She went to the wall, with her candle and her bees, unfastened the basket lid and watched. If she were not wrong they would all go to the same fissure in the wall. Searlait held her breath, the bee's progress would be quick, maybe too quick for her to follow. The bees rayed against the wall, buzzing madly, two stood guard, the others searching. She watched as they buried themselves into the sand at the base of the rock and disappeared.

Searlait shoved the candle into the goat skull and began digging in the soft sand. Almost panic took over her. The gift of water from the desert was not common, after her confrontation with the Sun God and escape from the vicious Wind; Searlait wanted to claim the life of this unexpected treasure. She dog paddled at the sand, digging furiously, when she fell, much more uncomfortably then her first entrance into this challenging haven.

Head first she rolled into an underground desert grotto, submersing into a pool of sweet water. She struggled at first to find ground, gasping for air, in an ungainly dance. The pool was man made, lined in precisely cut black stone. Searlait stood up washing herself in a childish joy. She tried to swim, and laughed out loud, sucking water through every air passage. as she coughed and sputtered and floundered, not relinquishing any joy to discomfort. Searlait ended sitting straight up in water a meter deep, legs fanned out in front of her, her veils, gossamer sheets riding above her hips. She still stammered giggles, scooping water in her cupped hands over her head. She could see the light from the cave above her head; her makeshift candle was shuddering.

Searlait removed herself from the pool and stripped off her veils. She climbed the wall to her unexpected entrance, and retrieved her goat skull. It was hot; she juggled it slightly till she set it down. She became instantly aware of her nakedness in the light, and how rare and precious it had become. She took in the cave.

Crafted from ancient hands, this cave was never meant to be entered. It was a shrine of pure wonder. Each stone lined wall held several sconce's punctuated with antiquated lamps. Strange murals adorned each wall, colorful, but stark with angled corners and stoic procession. An altar bearing a stone god, with a human face sat on the farthest wall, a god in prayer. The pool was perfectly circular and smooth, cunningly made to reflect the cave. On the ceiling was a starry shape. Searlait did not know, but it was the Egyptian Goddess Nut, in perfect calm, enduring her mundane duty of swallowing and giving birth to the sun.

Searlait spent two days inside the cavern. Reading the painted wall, deciphering the pictures with her own short knowledge. She timidly lit the lamps, one at a time. The starry goddess that reigned above changed with each lamp, the sun moving through her with the compliance of a child. She could feel the movement in her own body. The dark swallow, the ripeness in the growing belly, and the birth of the full sun, painless and sweet, a gentle transition of time. Searlait had not thought of the sun as a child, emerging new and gentle from a formed powerful woman, this was the mother of the sun. Taking him in and allowing him rest, nourishing him, waking him to his Day. The Sun God had a mother, and she was God.

On the second day Searlait broke the goat skull, and tattooed herself in the starry pattern of the Mother God over her heart center. She became the Mother God. She would not answer to the Sun, she was the parent. She would be the guide; she would take the power of her own life. Searlait became a revolutionary.

Early in the morning of the third day, Searlait climbed out of the cavern naked, one gauzy blue veil covering her head. Another of her veils she tied to a stone at the entrance to the cave. The submissive stars were still anchored in their homes, looking down at her with wonder; she turned east. The journey would not be far. At sunrise she should be among her tribe. Searlait was bursting with the power of her revelation. She dreamed of bringing her people back to the cavern and thrusting her conversion at them. They would see what she now thought of as "what she had always known". Searlait had twisted her vision of who she was, with a nagging religious doubt, that truthfully she had never had. Her revelation had freed her from her veils, and at the same time created an excuse for her to have used them.

The air and sand were still as Searlait made her journey to the east. The Wind was hiding and Searlait knew that he felt her power and cowered in some withering canyon. The Moon was racing to the horizon; the sister of the Sun God sensed the coming conflict and hurried to be out of sight. The stars were fading in the blue gold of twilight. She hurried into the path of the Sun.

The Gens D'Etoile would be waiting for the sun, weary from a night of playing under the stars. Families would be gathering together for the morning pray. Like disobedient children they slept while their God rode in the sky. His presence overwhelming the day with his attentive eye they moved in the darkness of the stars. Still adhering to his bidding, they told themselves, they moved while he slept and captured a bit of autonomy, cool, soft blue freedom from his heat. The Gens D'Etoile were coupled with the stars, the family they had left behind, perhaps some had been lovers or confidants, they were caught in a net of punishment, to be part of God's order or to share in the banishment. The Gens D'Etoile lived in both worlds, serving their time of punishment and rejoicing with their counterparts in the darkness.

Searlait kicked the sand with her bare feet. She felt gracious and poised gussied with newfound power. As darkness left the sky she approached the camp. Her tent was undisturbed, the hives humming in stacks of woven palm made her think of work that needed to be done. She had been gone a long time. There were other more important matters that needed to be attended to first. Searlait went straight to her mother's tent and called out to her. "Mere c'est Searlait". She knew her father would not acknowledge her any longer. They had not spoken since she had left their home. The tent was tied with soft strips of fabric from the inside. Not a wisp of wind moved beneath the tent, all was silent and still. Searlait looked beyond their tent. The children were absent. The Gens D'Etoile camp was empty. No voice or movement rippled the empty circle. Women should have been strolling openly in their beauty, giving anticipation to the ending of the Morning Prayer. The men should be sitting in repose, their eyes naked with future thoughts. They were gone. The camp was deserted.

Searlait called out, "Bonjour Gens D'Etoile". Her revelation still surging through her, she had never wanted to share anything but this, with these, her people, and its impact was being stolen from her. The Gens D'Etoile were gone.

The Sun God must have sulked and fumed while

Searlait uncovered his truths. In humiliation he stole the Gens D'Etoile from the earth, before they could know of his carefully concealed identity. Searlait went to each tent, she knew each home, and it felt strange to wander amongst them where she had not been welcomed. The fires were cold; no food had been cooked that night, or the day before. The Sun God had wasted no time in scooping up his prisoners and setting them in the sky. Searlait could only imagine the lies that he told them, the promises, the patronizing forgiveness. As the cowardly God crested the sand, Searlait stood and stared at his childish roundness, still shimmering wet from his mother's womb. He was happy, like a child who has gotten his way after a fitful tantrum. There was an air of indifference about his demeanor, he was not looking at Searlait any longer, he was humming to himself, caught in his own day, stubbornly riding across the sky with his eye turned upward, avoiding her gaze. Searlait went to her own tent and slept in the security of the familiar past.

That evening she waited for the stars. They began to peer out, one by one from the darkling sky. She called out their names as they appeared, and spoke greetings to them, waiting for the newly placed stars to show themselves. She knew where each Gens D'Etoile should be placed. The Water Dipper should have a cascade of stars flowing from one to the next. The lion's mane would be full and furious. Searlait's Mother would be shining in the smile of the great Virgin, next to her father, a tear on the Virgin's cheek. The sky broke into blue darkness, with its curtain of diamonds glistening in the stillness. The stars of the Gens D'Etoile did not appear new and prosperous, the dark space had not changed, the long promise was unkept.

    Searlait slept. She woke while the child Sun was rushing to his mother's lips. She did not acknowledge his presence, but gathered a few of her belongings. Feeling vulnerable and alone, she chose to wrap herself in the dark veils that her mother used when she traded with de la Terre. She borrowed her mother's sandals and dressed her veils with her jewelry. A small hive would travel on her head, the rest of the hives she opened, thanked the bees for sharing their lives with her and stood as they swarmed around her and disappeared into the desert. She packed honey and fresh goat's cheese into palm leaves. A bladder of water, and a small rug to sleep on completed her stores. The Gens D'Etoile had traveled as far East as they were known to, within the next day they would have begun the northwest journey. The small river, Larmoyent Argent, was not far and de la Terre would be on its banks.

    Searlait's solitary journey would take her back and forth across the desert. She became a phantom thief to survive, living in the dark, taking refuge from the sunlit sky. Between the tribes of the de la Terre the myth of a veiled queen that took small offerings of food followed her over the wasteland. Searlait was still the same, her existence shrouded and secretive, layered with loneliness and abandonment. She leaned on long ago dreams of kindness unknown and wondered where she was and when she would be found.

The Enchantment

The desert has an unerring loneliness to its existence. Every creature seems to live in solitude. The lizard, the snake, the scorpion, the cactus. A musky allure draws them to one another for a single moment of companionship that will seal the seamlessness of their life to the next. Only the mammals live in-groups of maternal love and playful fathers, not the most prolific of the desert dwellers, or the most successful, but who is to say not the most contented. Where ever love is offered, it must be as sweet as bee's honey.

Searlait had two journeys' around the sun and the desert was savoring the consuming of her. She had not spoken to another person since she had left the Gens D'Etoile to scavenge in the desert. She had lived on the fringe of tribes, stealing into their camps in the darkness, a shadow. Searlait felt protected by the great goddess. But her veils were now thin and fading, she was beginning to fade. Her tiny frame was now that of a child's and she grew thinner by the day. Her conscience would not allow her to outright steal food without leaving something in return, so bit by bit her mother's jewelry was offered in compensation. She did not know that the rumor of her appearance spread throughout the tribes. Myths of the phantom goddess became a measure of good omen if she took an offering, children begged to put things out for her, but it was the women who left the most.

Searlait kept to the old track of the Gens D'Etoile for the first year of her solitude, hoping to find her family, like a gift precious and unexpected, just as they were, but accepting and joyous to see her. This was her dream, but the trek was more difficult then she remembered. When she came to their final camp, just as it was, wind torn and empty. The Gens D'Etoile were gone. Searlait turned west into the unknown.

Eventually she made her way towards the sea, where breezes cooled the blistering sun and life gathered on its pink beaches. Instinct led her way through the unfamiliar savannah to the groaning roar of the ocean. Searlait's first encounter with the huge heaving sea was in moonlight, shimmering blue and frosted with golden waves. It's powerful voice was inescapable and its size intimidating. She sat on the cool, damp sand and could not comprehend this foreign power, no sun ruled this force. Searlait had found another God, and she sat at his feet.

By morning Searlait was retreating back to the savannah. The presence of the ocean left her head pounding and numb, the unfamiliar coolness seemed to seep it's way under her veils, leaving her clammy and cold, she thought this God was coming up right out of the sand to envelop her in his powerful grasp. She had not decided if this God was good or harsh, she would reserve judgment until she could learn more. Searlait needed to regroup with familiar landscapes, after being in the presence of the ocean God. It was exhausting and she found her heart beating hard and her breath coming in short gasps. Fear was not common for Searlait; not this fear, and she left the blue beast crawling on the shore searching for her.

For a day Searlait journeyed inland. She slept little and walked while the Sun traveled the sky. She felt him laughing at her, running from a power that she knew he understood. The Sun gained much pleasure at her fear; she did her best to ignore his stare. She grew weak and trembled with hunger, but she read this as an aftermath condition of the sea's great power. Even from a great distance she could still hear the ocean's voice in her head and the strength leaving her legs.

Searlait passed the huts of the Azure women in pure darkness of early night and found a path following a shallow gentle river. It's constant gurgle was sweet and calming, she drank from it and felt refreshed, the voice of the ocean had left her ears, and the air was dry and warm. Far from the huts Searlait stopped and watched the sister Moon rise from the ground. Full and gleaming white, casting Searlait in shadowed light; she greeted her with relief, a tranquil and intimate strength that filled Searlait with a feeling of reprieve. She could rest here, the moon glowing bright, with a blue iridescent veil around her shoulders, the river caught this light and tiny stars gleamed from its surface. Searlait was home; she imagined the tiny points of light as her family and for a moment allowed herself to believe that they were. She removed her veils and bathed in the gift of their presence. Her last thought was that she would wash her veils in the morning and allow the sun to dry them for her, and she collapsed into the river, naked, starving, lonely, and about to be found.

Ioman still kept watch on the river, although not as diligent as in the first years after the war. The solitude of his home created a comfortable peace. On the night that Searlait stole into the boundaries of their river home Ioman had an uneasy feeling and had taken up watch. The smooth, oily darkness of the early night had insisted on his presence. His thoughts would not allow sleep, and an uneasy restlessness called him to one of his lookouts.

The river was a dark, velvety line that bubbled, almost silent, against the darkness of the banks. It was a perfect night for invasion. As the moon rose Ioman's instincts were heighten. Did he see men poised to attack from the opposite shore? No, only rocky spear points, that he knew well. His mind dreamed of lurking enemies, it seemed every sense in his body was tense to discovery. And then he smelled something. There was a scent on the river, salty-sweet, the ocean stirred with melted honey, and his groin started to ache. His intuit became acute, his eyes tried to come out of his face to see the darkness, his ears grew to hear what was approaching and his hands became numb with want. Time became immeasurable, he breathed as one who was on a hunt; he waited for the moonrise.

At first moon glow over the plateau he spotted the small figure of Searlait. His view was obstructed, she had stopped too soon. It was a child and his mind raced. He thought of all the children of the Azures and wondered if it could be one of them. What would a child be doing here? His muscles became tense, his back arched and a growl seemed to escaped from depths he had not known before.

Frustrated by his poor vantage point, Ioman ducked into the tunnel that wound through his home and ran to the far end of the hideaway, to the very last chimney hole. The child was still too far, but his mind told him any distance, but directly underneath him would be too far. He watched with a stillness that belied his body.

Searlait stood poised and noble as she took in the moon. Ioman watched as she shed her veils, and he felt himself grow calm. She was a woman and a deep curious peace settled in his stomach. He watched as she bathed, pouring shimmering stars over her head, massaging her thighs and belly, she caressed herself with slow, tender attention. Ioman was captured by the spell, he lived in the moment with her, forgetting where he was, who he was before the gift of her had arrived. The spell broke as he saw her fold into the water and not move again.

The Azure Women

Ioman carried Searlait to his home and laid her in his bed. Reluctantly he covered her with his own cloths, and waited for her to awaken. He prepared a broth for her and stroked her head with his huge hands, all the while telling her the tale of his life. Searlait did not move, did not dream and did not awaken until the stars glowed in the night sky. Ioman was there, and when she opened her eyes all she could see was the huge dark face of the man she had envisioned all her life, and he smiled and was quiet. They had found each other.

Life moved as a dream for Ioman and Searlait, each moment a discovery, a new revelation, and a stream of unbroken moments totally immersed with each other. Their paths seemed to meld seamlessly into one new path, their old lives forgotten, as a distant wasteland of time that had not been spent together. Ioman's old enemies became an admission of something he had already conquered, and had long feared without justification. Searlait's long wanderings were only a path to Ioman, she could rest, laugh, eat, and smile, dream of nothing not found. For the two of them daily existence with each other was the only way life should have ever been. They did not consider that the Azure's would feel differently.

The Azures had faced many difficult changes in the last years, the most prominent being the focus and position of the Azure women. The power struggle within the society had created a grasping tension between the detached males and the demanding dominance of the females. Searlait's presence only heightens the tension for the women. The Azure men welcomed Searlait. Her exotic feminine beauty and docile attention entranced them. Searlait made each man feel they had captured a special place in her heart, she showed them gentle warmth and an individual respect, that had been common among the Gens D'Etoile, her power was drenched in honey and suckled from the softest breast. For the Azure women, she had stolen their warrior, the strong masculine jewel that had been just out of reach, but could still be lured for a moment by the right stare or sway of the hips. Soon Searlait showed the belly of a coming child. Now Ioman's eye never wandered from his heart. Searlait had become a queen with all its devoted attention and regal love, she was the measure by which each Azure man aspired.

Slowly the Azure men began to visit with their tribal woman, but their attention had dimmed and their demeanor had changed. The women became more demanding, feeling the emptiness of their visits. Searlait had been with Ioman for over a year, a moment of time for them, and an unbearable struggle for the Azure women. Then a breath of light showed itself, and the women convened to plan for an annual festival, in which they were the stars.

Careful planning went into the festival. Decorations were strung between the huts, dances were rehearsed, costumes constructed with exacting messages. It appeared colorful and festive, food and drink were hoarded, a labor of joy and excitement filled the village. The festival would take place during the length of the the moon's longest absence, under the brightest stars, and the darkest of night. With all the excitement, there was a silent undercurrent of jealousy and malice. If one looked closely, a hidden secret could be found in hooded eyes, and a suspicious knowing smirk, hiding in smiles.

A crescent moon still cast a blue light on the savanna, when a child approached Ioman's rock lookout. The son of one of the guards, he asked for his father. They had a hurried reunion, that ended with a plea to see Ioman. The boy unveiled a sinister plot. The festival was being used to end Searlait's life, and of the child that grew inside her. If the women did not succeed, it would not end, the boy said, their hatred had grown to deep.

Ioman stared at Searlait as she slept. They had not married, for Ioman it seamed redundant, he felt they were one, long before they had met. Now she lay there with his child. He would kill for this woman, every Azure woman if he had to. Searlait's condition made an escape problematic. A boat had already been summoned, they could take the river to the ocean. It would take them past the village, the men agreed to distract the Azure women during their festival, as they floated past. Perhaps a weak plan, but hastily organized for a hurried escape.

Searlait was not strong, the baby inside her was sapping her energy. The day of the festival dragged along. All we're waiting for nightfall. The Azure women were giddy with their pending deception, the men nervous in their ability to deceive them. The boat arrived, stocked with skins of water and a store of food. Blankets lined the floor and spears clung to the sides. Ioman tried his best to explain to Searlait, she would have to stay hidden in the boat. Strangely they seemed to communicate together, in their own way, that no one else could understand.

Twilight took a colorful stage, creating a backdrop of drama to the upcoming deception. Searlait took her place in the boat, she felt ungainly. Ioman was going to swim next to the boat, two of his men accompanied him, hopefully they would evade detection. The rest of the men made their way to the village, meeting a host of women on their way to the lookout, with the guise of welcoming Searlait to the celebration. They were told she was already on her way, and they should all travel to the village together. The men were jovial, smiling, playing with the women in a teasing, admiring fashion. The deceptions began.

The women had anticipated an escape. They knew what the men were up to. The Azure men didn't know the women had bargained with their enemies, the Lassana tribe they had long ago warred with, were waiting on the far bank of the river, to stage a takeover of the river path to the sea. No one foresaw that the Azure women would bond with their enemies, who were now young and strong, their hearts full of revenge. The women were done with the entranced Azure men. The depth of their hatred unanticipated, the Azure men were unarmed, and naive, when it came to just what the women were capable of.

The Lassana were placed, as the Azure women had planned with them. They had no interest in their petty jealousies, or that they felt wronged and discarded by their men. The Lassana had their own women, their own ways and wanted the passage to the sea. The final deception was about to unfold. And the ambush began.

Ioman's boat slid in the darkness across from the village. The festival appeared joyful, dancing and drumming filled the air. Torches burned, while a single voice rang out with the call of the hyena, all the women took up the call, and the Lassana attacked. The Azure women attacked their own men, singing turned into screams, the Lassana took to the river. They ignored Ioman's boat and made their way to the shore. Other enemy forces were staged inland beyond the village, unknown to the Azure women.

As the Azure people were about to be annihilated, stars started to fall from the sky. Ioman was yelling orders to his men, he armed the two men with spears, and ordered the men to get their children out of the village. Searlait lay helpless in the commotion, then sat up, staring at the night sky. She stood, transfixed by the heavens, the stars had started to move, and Searlait began to sing.

Her voice rang out, there were no words, just notes. Undulating, eerily beckoning. Rising in welcome, then humble in its offering. Challenging and harsh, falling to a soft cooing. As she sang the stars falling became more intense and violent. Spears were raining on the fray, in blue explosions of fiery smoke. Columns of cloud appeared beyond the stars, dark blue, swirling grey and smoky, a rosy glow promised violence. Every movement stopped for uncomprehending moments. Searlait was commanding the stars. Her arms raised in hopeful reunions, she stood as a goddess, pregnant with glory. In a sudden movement the Lassana retreated to the east, the Azure women scattered to the huts. Ioman shocked, but still focused, used the moment to push the boat through the narrow crevice to the sea.

As they slipped into a glassy, smooth sea, Searlait collapsed into the boat, holding her belly. Ioman used one paddle to get them as far as he could from the shore. He looked back, his heart ached to fight. Ioman had to let go of his old life, of course that had happened the first time he had embraced Searlait. The sky became calm, and Ioman soon laid down with Searlait, together they fell into an uneasy sleep.

The current of the sea took it's passengers into the darkness. Ioman woke to Searlait moaning, cradling her belly and curling into a ball of pain. Waves rocked the boat wickedly, while Ioman tried to comfort Searlait with water from a skin. The sun came up and went down with indifference to his dilemma, Searlait's screams of pain were hair raising as she clutched at her back and at her groin. The dark night went on and on for what seemed a never ending confinement, and an unbearable lack of relief. Searlait motioned for Ioman to cut her, she drew a line on her belly with a shacking hand, between what were shattering screams that would never leave the one who heard it.

As shadowed light came into the sky, Ioman broke the

one spear he had from its shaft and motioned for Searlait to lay still. His voice loud and commanding, Searlait had tried to climb out of the boat several times, and he had been gruff and harsh in his efforts to restrain her. With the spear tip he cut her belly, as she had indicated. He was reminded of an antelope kill, he believed he was taking her life. Tears ran from his eyes, he looked at Searlait and she nodded yes, and laid still, as he made the incision.

He could see the round shape of the baby's head, he grabbed the neck and drew him from his mother's womb. A thick membrane sack encased him, Ioman used the spear tip to break him free, in a cascade of fluid the baby took his first breath. He laid the baby on Searlait's bare chest and wrapped them in a blanket, while he tended to Searlait. He took her head scarf and wrapped the incision tightly, bent her knees to her belly. Searlait was either unconscious or asleep, he told himself, hoping, beyond hope, that she was alive. Ioman knelt at her feet, his eyes closed and he collapsed holding the side of the boat.

The Lifted Veil

The shore of Gobelin was quiet that morning, the tide was low. So low, the white sand stretched out as a pristine walk under the sea. This low tide was uncommon, all things had come together to bring it's bounty within reach. Aage was at the shore that morning, taking advantage of the gifts to be found. With her feet sugared in sand, she gathered fresh seaweed, scallop shells, sea glass, several conch shell, filled with its delicious host. All the winking treasures lay vulnerable, and naked. Aage worked diligently, dragging as much as she could to the beach, she knew her time was short. The feminine of the sea was exposed and offering. The breeze was luscious and warm, stirring lovely gentle passion. As the sun started to rise, Aage saw the fire, red and irritated, wrapped in shredded, blood red clouds. It would mean rain and winds later in the day. And the tide would surge back soon to reclaim its beach. Aage felt she had ventured to far. It was time to take her stolen treasure to the shoreline, when she spotted a boat. It was at the retracted shoreline, against her own judgment, Aage ran towards it. This was a find she couldn't pass by, she could leave the island, venture into the sea, a boat brought so many possibilities, just the things she could use the wood for already argued in her mind. As she got close, she slowed when she realized the boat came with a man. She could see his head bent over the side, asleep perhaps. Boy was the last person she had seen, and that had been years ago. No one had come to the island, she had spent her whole life in solitude. She stood numb, unable to move. Ioman opened his eyes and looked directly at her.

What he saw was an apparition. A tall, wisp of a woman, with white hair as long as she stood tall. Her dress was white, small shells were woven into the breast plate. She seemed almost transparent, but glowed with shimmering color. His first thought was of a spirit, an angel, come to help him. He moved slowly, afraid she would disappear. His feet touched the sand and he spoke to her. His hands in prayer, his voice pleading. "Makaila, Makaila!" He slowly approached her, his voice streaming his need. Tears ran from his eyes. He stopped before he reached her, pointing back to the boat, his open hand beating his chest, begging for help.

Aage could not understand his voice or words. It sounded like a song, her memory briefly flickered back to church hymns. He needed help, that she understood. He was the biggest man she had ever seen, he had a beauty and a strength that was beckoning. She moved towards him, she couldn't look away from him. As she reached him, his stream of song grew as she arrived at the boat. Aage realized there was something in the boat he wanted her to see, she finally broke her gaze and looked into the boat. A woman and a newborn child lay in the bottom. Ioman did his best to tell her what had happened. Aage took this all in and motioned to Ioman to get the boat to the beach. Aage looked back at the sea, white sea foam rose out of the water. The pending moment of being overtaken by the sea was at hand. Ioman read it in her face, the fear looked like a sickness on her. Together they tried to push the boat, the wet sand resisted their efforts. The sea would not wait. They were violently overturned by a rouge wave from the side.

Aage was knocked off her feet, she was tossed carelessly, her head hit something hard, her basket ripped from her shoulder, her hair became a stranglehold leaving her incapacitated, helpless, drowning as she fought to get to the surface. Then just darkness.

It was mid morning when Aage woke, coughing, choking on sand and tangled in her own hair. Ioman was there by her side. He spoke calling her Bibi, he moved her hair from around her neck, he was asking if she were alright and pointed to Searlait and the baby next to her. Aage sat up. Her head spinning. Aage needed to gather all that had happened. The boat had been taken in the waves, Ioman had saved them all with quick wits, sheer desire, and the pure strength of defiance. The moments lived like hours in his memory. When Aage opened her eyes, Ioman was trying to tend to Searlait. Ioman tried to tell Aage he was overjoyed she was still alive, but concerned it was just barely. His love for them laid bare in his face, his voice, and movements. Aage had to take them to her home.

Gobelin had served Aage well over the years. The island had always provided as Aage needed things. Her home had become very comfortable. Boy had collected the white fibers that collected in the sea grass to make wicks for candles. Aage continued after he left. She spun and knotted the strands and years of blankets, pillows, floor covers, curtains, clothes cluttered her home. Aage had so much honey she stored it in the same wax vials Boy had designed so many years ago, and stacked them to make walls between the cooking and sleeping room. The rooms still rained candles. There was a tiny stove outside to cook fish and eggs, flat bread and soup. Together she and Boy had built the shell that created the outside walls, mostly rock and mud.

When the shipwrecked survivors arrived in Aage's home, Aage had Ioman wait till she could light candles and showed him her bed where he place Searlait. It was the same tiny nutshell boat Aage had arrived in so many years ago. Now it overflowed with downy stuffed pillows and blankets. The room's glowed through honey vials. The tiny flowers suspended in wax came to life and played a charming game in the flickering flames. Aage took to tending Searlait right away. She gave her a vial of honey brew to ease her pain. For the baby she made a sucking cloth, tiny amounts of chamomile and lavender dipped in honey water. She cleaned the incision on Searlait's belly and stitched it closed with a strand of her hair. When Searlait was resting and Aage had applied a poultice of sea grass and honey to her belly, she took the baby gently from Ioman and placed him with his mother to suckle. When all was quiet, Aage brought them both a vial of the honey brew she had learned to make so long ago.

Ioman and Aage sat on the floor allowing the brew to work it's warming magic. Searlait was in a deep sleep. All will be alright, she told him, Boy will be home soon and all things would be good. Ioman didn't understand, but he read the tone in her voice and the relaxed slouch in her shoulders. He agreed with her, yes Bibi, he nodded.

There was a small bed Aage had fashioned for Boy, it sat undisturbed waiting for his return. Ioman patted the soft cushion and pointed to Aage, rest he motioned. Ioman didn't know Aage's reverence for the things she had made for Boy, but Ioman's demeanor was to be obeyed. It made sense to him and there would be no question. He gently lay next to Searlait , "Ndoto ." He whispered "dream." They all fell into a family sleep, the kind that embraces being safe and loved, not even thinking of tomorrow's promise.

There was a comfortable familiarity with the four of them. Life seamlessly took on the patter of mundane warmth. Searlait recovered under the watchful eye of Aage and the two women became sister like, their shared love for honey was an easy friendship. They tended Aage's gardens together. Aage grew soft and almost, almost became loving. Ioman took to work, he decided they would all live together, he set to building rooms for he and Searlait. They named their son Levian, he had his mother's coloring, and his father's structure. He had the beautiful face of the Gens D'Etoile women, and the infectious smile of the Azures. He was the perfect blend of his parents.

Moments turned into months, and then a year. When a boat arrived from the east. The three of them watched as it anchored and men came ashore. Ioman turned to the women, raised a finger, and went to approach them.

They were Spaniard's on their way home and stopped to replenish water and any meat, or fruit that may be available. They were traders.

On Ioman's return he told the women. He made a decision to trade honey and would return the next day. They gave him a cart and some wooden crates. That night they listened to the jovial Spaniard's laughing and singing, drinking around an open fire.

Ioman discussed with Searlait and Aage how they felt about trading with these men. Aage was distrustful and suspicious. That was her nature, Ioman assured her they would leave and her home would not be detected. Searlait had always traded in her past and helped Ioman convince Aage. They packed the cart with vials of honey and clay pots of honey brew. That morning they watched as Ioman dragged the cart to the eastern beach. Aage still apprehensive, Searlait put her arm around her and whispered assurances, and they waited for Ioman's return.

It was sundown when Ioman returned, dragging the same cart, loaded with the bounty he had collected. Ioman had waited till the Spaniard's were on board and had set sail, before he left the shore. In return for the honey he had acquired several small metal pots There were spices, and a small amount of rice. Ioman had gifts as well, veils for Searlait adorned with silver charms and combs for Aage's hair, carved out of abalone imbedded with tiny pearls. But the most special was a mirror.

Both of the women were uneasy looking into the mirror,

but Levian couldn't stop laughing at himself in it, he tried to grab his own hand and face over and over. He examined his ears, his eyes and nose, ran his fingers over his sparse hair. He made everyone laugh, that made him "child angry". But it would be forgotten quickly. It took a short time for Levian to decide he was very good looking. He brought his mother's face close to his to examine their faces together. The mirror proved to be better than any toy he could have been given.

So their lives thrived. Boats would come and go laden with the beautiful honey. Eventually some of the sailors brought their wives, or families and wanted to stay. A small township sprang up, complete with cobblestone streets and shops, a tavern, a church. The harbor had wooden piers. It bustled with laughter and arguments and moved with commerce. The hives of Aage lay hidden, no one ventured to explore the western corner. There was a rumor that a witch lived there, the newcomers told their children. The solitary existence of Aage was protected. Aage suspected Ioman and she thanked him. The years would pass peacefully. Gobelin had welcomed this group, but magic is funny. Unknowable really, perhaps one could say untrustworthy.

The Illuminist

An ocean away a man walked on a wooden pier. He was tall and straight. His hair dark and long, his beard full, he lit a wooden pipe. He ignored the drizzle of rain and the fog, that the gaslight lamps could not penetrate. The wharf was busy, sailors were disembarking from their trading ships, glad to touch land and rest. The man was making his way to the Witches Promise tavern. They served beef chunks in rich gravy alongside fried potatoes that he had a yearning for. The Witches Promise was busy, but not so busy, the man couldn't take a seat right away, and waited, enjoying his pipe. The stone fireplace roared with fire. Candlelight attempted to penetrate the darkness of the dreary wharf, that seeped through the walls. The assembly of men gathered in the tavern were glad to be off a ship. They shared their stories and laughter, along side a much deserved draft of brew. A barmaid brought the lone man a pint of beer.

"Ahh, Claret you are my heart's desire." He feigned sovereignty.

"The usual?" She replied dispassionately.

He nodded and she turned abruptly, happy to leave him to his beer and alone. He appeared deep in thought, a dower look on his face when a sailor appeared at his table side.

"My friend! Illuminati! May I sit with you my friend?"

A nod allowed his wish. His name was Quisan. A long legged sailor with a wife and children. Quisan was happy on the sea.

"You would not believe the trade my friend! We are floating away with money, it makes the work seem that less."

The barmaid appeared with a pint of beer, "anything else?"

"What he's having."

"How have you been, how has life treated you?" Quisan implored.

"The journey has been arduous, as life can be."

"You have no wife, my friend, you need a wife."

"You hate your wife, why wish that on myself?" The man replied.

Two plates of food arrived, unceremoniously served, the cutlery a loud accompaniment.

"More beer my love." Quisan half asked in his broken accent.

"This is true, I hate my wife, but naked she is a soft, a willing pillow of sanctuary. I can lose myself in the folds of her breasts, the sweet smoke…"

"Alright, enough, I know why you have so many children."

Quisan grinned, proudly showing missing teeth, scooping gravy and meat with abandon. He waves at Claret, "Bread, please?" He shouted, above the voices.

"I hate my wife, but always bring her a gift, she will

be happy when I return." Quisan reached into his bag and brought out a vial of honey, he sat it on the table in front of the Illuminist.

Summer danced in front of him, sweet flowers preserved in the wax promised the essence of scent. The Illuminist mind raced to memories of his youth. The vial glistened in the flickering light of the fire.

"Where did you get this?" The Illuminist demanded adamantly.

Bread appeared on the table and Quisan ordered another plate, he pointed to his friend and he shook his head no.

"The bread is cold." Quisan stated. He picked up the vial and turned it with thick fingers. "This comes from Gobelin, it is worth more than gold. Dame Miel makes the best honey in the known world, my friend. I took this as payment for passage on this last leg."

"What is Gobelin? Where is it?" The question was direct.

"Is an island on the trade routes, not easy to find. A ship leaves tomorrow bound for its shore, making three port stops, a hard tour. Gobelin the last, but the brew, ahh, my friend, it is warm enchantment. Well worth the effort." Quisan saw the desire in his friend's face, he picked up the vial and placed it back in his bag. The summer light was extinguished.

The Illuminist heard the door slam as he left the Witches Promise. He walked out into the fog. He lit his pipe. His memory drew him back to Aage, and his short life with her on the island, he had fought thoughts of that time his whole life. The vial of honey could have been one he made. The ray of hives surrounding the tiny house. The warm days that seemed to have lasted forever, filled with sweet flowers and white sand beaches. His memory would not allow him to dismiss the beauty.

The Illuminist booked passage that night on The Astarte. A merchant ship, not a hard leg, but a full year at sea. It would be laborious work, he was use to hard work. It didn't matter, now he wanted to see Aage. If she were still alive, if she would see him. If she remembered him, he was her son. He asked himself if he remembered his mother, and if she had been a mother. He hadn't thought of her as a mother. He grew to be a man, without a name.

Five months into the journey the ship anchored off Greybarr. A tiny bit of island that had little to trade but wool. No one was allowed to go ashore, just a small contingent to negotiate the trade. The Illuminist was approached by the Captain, Captain Marcel Cabot, "You look just like these people, do you know them? They are hard, just like you, will you come ashore?"

He agreed, anything to get off the ship, if only for a short time. When they landed, he thought it odd that only a small circle of men met them. The island felt deserted, but for these few men, they were ushered into a conclave attached to the church, and offered only a seat. All of the men were eerily similar. The negotiations were short, the Greybarr men tried to amplify their position, drawing the discussions out with long convoluted arguments. Captain Cabot granted them this respect. They were allowed to think what they had to trade was truly valuable, water and wool. In truth Cabot felt sorry for these people, they were isolated, he assumed they rarely had a chance to spout the pent up voices that gave them self importance. There was one man at the table who seemed to be the loudest, elder voice. The Illuminist asked him, "Our men have been at sea for a long journey, could they come ashore, just to stretch their legs."

"There is nothing here for the men to occupy their minds with. We have been attacked by sorcery in the past, the evil underbelly that threaten to undermine the Almighty God that rules us all. My own daughter turned evil before my very eyes. We cannot risk Witchery and entrapment to ensnare us in its web!" His speech was long, a story this old man told himself, a justification, or a confession? Or a lie? The Illuminist looked deeply into his face, he could have been looking into a mirror. Not his words, his face, his hands, his hairline, his eyes. The old elder was not smart, shut off from the world was not sophisticated in debate. He had said too much and didn't know it. The Illuminist interrupted to ask another question "My pardons sir, may I ask what became of your daughter?"

"She was punished, banished from this place so she may not bewitch another, we are God Fearing, righteous men!" His voice rose, his arms animated his anger. He kept speaking, the justification for the punishment hammered into the table he stood in front of.

In a pause, the Illuminist asked another question, "Whom did your daughter bewitch?"

A long silence accompanied a cold stare.

"Gentlemen, we have gotten off topic, have we come to an agreement? I believe we have completed the negotiations and all contracts can be signed." The tempered voice of

Captain Cabot concluded the session.

The elder Greybarr stood frozen in his stare, that answered the Illuminist question more than any words.

It was a long night for the Illuminist, he did the math, he dreamed of Aage, he pictured her pain. He heard words she had never meant to speak, nightmares she wouldn't remember. He had to have the answer. He was convinced the elder was his father, and Aage's father as well. It churned in his stomach. He stole off the ship and took the small boat used to ferry back and forth to the island. He knocked on the first door he saw. He explained he needed to speak with the elder, there was a problem with the trade, he explained. The sleepy eyed man told him where to find him. He went to the elder's door and banged loudly. A woman answered, the Illuminist asked to speak with the elder, it was urgent he explained. He was ushered in and waited.

"What is this urgency?" The old man asked, woke out of sleep, disturbed, he fussed with the tie of his robe as he took a seat. The Illuminist was in no mood for inconvenient apologies or pretext to given importance.

"Was your daughter's name Aage?" The Illuminist asked calmly.

"What? How do you know that name? Who do you think you are to come here at this time of night? What are you accusing me of?" The old man became very angry, quickly. He was coming out of his chair.

" I am her son. I thought you might like to know."

The old man stood, the Illuminist stood, he drew a blade and slit his father's throat, pushed him back into the chair. Wiped his blade on the old man's robe and quietly let himself out, he returned to the ship.

Once again he would awakened someone from sleep. Cabot listened to the Illuminist story. "The ship is loaded, we leave now. Wake the men, tell them to be quiet. I'll set the course for Gobelin."

And the Illuminist was on course to see Aage.

The Astarte dropped anchor in the crumbling harbor of Gobelin at sundown. The Illuminist took in the cobblestone street with a wary eye, the wooden deck looked waterlogged and spongy. He made his way down the gangplank, hesitant and wary. The island had changed, he walked looking for something familiar. He wondered if this had been the island he had been born on. He was a stranger here. He reached the western corner and saw the hives. Slowly he approached. The bees were humming in their hives. The scent of honey hung in the air. He had a memory of how it should be, there was something different, a musk, echos of movement that excluded him. All traces of himself were gone. The Illuminist questioned his wisdom on returning here. He had nothing with him, he hadn't thought to bring Aage a gift. With hesitation, a nervous feeling of doubt in his stomach of his acceptance here. He knocked on Aage's door, it opened, to his surprise at his touch and he walked in.

Captain Cabot watched as the Illuminist left. He ordered his crew to stay aboard. The murder on Greybarr put the entire ship in danger. He had no doubt the authorities would be looking for his ship. The men of Greybarr would shout and insist on justice. He could hear it, the opportunity to be acknowledged and important would not be foregone. There would be summons and inquiries. Possibly a trial. Hopefully he could leave the Illuminist and claim ignorance. Let him hang. He had no love for the man, he felt for his plight, but not the headache he brought upon himself. The Astarte would load without hesitation. His meeting with the wharf master was short, the contracts were agreed upon and signed. The exchange was expedited. Cabot was a smart man, The Astarte would set sail before midnight.

The crew grumbled angrily at not getting port time. Some threatened to leave, two legs without port! This was Gobelin! Shouts and protests broke out. A festival was planned! The men looked forward to companionship, the warm embrace of a woman perhaps, the honey brew of Gobelin, the laughter and indulgence of roasted meats and drink. Cabot was asking too much, as much as the crew respected the captain. They demanded an explanation.

"I know you are disappointed. I'm disappointed as well. Circumstances beyond my control deem it necessary that we leave immediately. I wish I could divulge the import. Knowledge would, or could implicate you." Captain Cabot addressed his crew.

He spoke to the men with as much honesty as he could. His voice convinced them that haste was necessary. Rumor's ran through the ship. They all knew the Illuminist had left. A shadowy questionable character at best. They assumed what ever charted the course had something to do with him. The Astarte set sail just before midnight for Spain. The men were promised full passage and a commission on the haul, upon docking in Spain. The wheel house predicted a five day journey, with Gods blessing of a smooth sea. The sails were hoisted, the fenders lifted and in the darkness the Astarte slid into the sea. With out the Illuminist.

Leaving only The Marchand at dock

The Beckoning

It had been a long day. A good day. Aage and Searlait had tended to the gardens and gathered honey, as they did. They waited for Ioman to return from the town they now shared the island with. Searlait called Aage her "star sister." Aage had learned to laugh and smile. The evening was pleasant .They watched the sun set. It would be a moonless night. Aage said she was tired and dinner still needed to be prepared, she went inside their home. She lit the candles and busied herself with the night's meal. A knock on the door caught her attention.

"Aage, it's Boy I've come to see you. Aage?" The Illuminist stepped over the threshold. The room looked magical, it moved with honeyed flowers, he had forgotten the sweet beauty, if he had ever really seen it before. It had changed, but held a semblance of the home he remembered.

"Aage? It's Boy."

"Boy?" The child that had occupied her mind for much of her life, that she had waited for, that she had looked for, that she was angry with. In an odd way Aage had used Boy as a vague protector, someone who may have even loved her, given her value. Over the years she had concocted stories in her imagination to bring him back to her. It had filled a loneliness for her, that would have been unbearable on it's own. On his return something crumbled in her reality, she was not ready for the real Boy.

"I look like your father Aage, don't be afraid."

Aage peered around the wall of honey vials that separated their voices.

"It's all right Aage, I know what I look like, I'm not here to hurt you." It was several minutes before either spoke. Aage stared at the man with suspicion. He did look like her father. Her heart beating loudly.

"Why are you here? What do you want?" Aage asked defensively.

"I heard about your honey." She looked so small he thought. "Can we sit? Just talk for a bit." The Illuminist found a kindness in himself he did not expect. Aage seemed so fragile, her eyes wide, her defenses peaked.

"Ioman will be here soon, Searlait she is here, she will come in anytime now." Her voice cracked with uncertainty, and a false bravado held back tears.

"Come and sit with me woman." He sat in the nearest chair. "You have made changes, the rooms are bigger, it's nice."

"Ioman did that, he will be here soon. You're sitting in his chair." She declared. His resemblance to her father churned in her stomach.

"You have done well Aage, your honey is famous, it travels the known world." The Illuminist kept his voice soft, as unthreatening as he could.

"I don't know about that, how could that be?" Aage dismissed the compliment.

"I want nothing from you. I just wanted to see you." He wondered why he had come. The meeting was awkward. They didn't know each other. "I was told you make honey brew?"

"It's a lot of work, too much for one person. Not enough hands for everything that needs to be done." Nervously she still stood across the room.

"Perhaps we could share a cup together. It has been a long time Mother."

Hearing him call her mother jarred in Aage's core, "Yes, we should, the first night Ioman and Searlait were here we had the honey brew." She was already in motion and brought it sheepishly. "I made this myself, it takes a long time, it's a lot of work."

"I know it's a lot of work, you have done so well." After a few sips. "This is very good. Thank you for sharing with me." Aage sat opposite the man.

"You left me." Aage said quietly. Trying to sound strong, angry even, she fell short.

"I did, I have asked myself if that were right or wrong many times. I needed to experience the world." He tried to explain. "I never meant to hurt you." Silence.

"You never gave me a name. I understand now why, perhaps you could try to understand why I left." Silence passed.

"I came here to tell you something." The Illuminist felt their time was coming to an end.

"What?" She said, her protective shield growing smaller in her mind.

"I spoke with my father." He waited to see how she would react. "I know what he did to you. I know all of it." Aage's hands started to shake, she didn't cry, but her paper thin cheeks were wet with tears. "I know it may not matter to you, but he was fraught with guilt, he punished himself with an angry life." He almost smiled thinking about their meeting. "You have lived a sublime life of solitude, you may not think so. But you have been blessed to live away from Greybarr. Any of the woman on Greybarr would change places with you if they could." They sat quietly together. He stood, picked up her hand, "You can rest now. Our father was dead when I left." Aage lifted his hand and held it to her cheek.

Night had fallen when The Illuminist left, a single vial of honey and a skin of honey brew went with him. A gift from his Mother. She had called him Son. Aage took their cups to the kitchen. Somehow she felt settled. The past was fading, the anger, the solitude. She looked around her home and felt blessed for the first time. She had been blessed with Boy, blessed with Searlait and Ioman, and Levian. The mirror still stood in its corner, its memories made her smile. Her bed, it was the same small nutshell of a boat she had arrived in, she had been an innocent young girl, who had been so brave. Now that boat was filled with softness and comfort. She laid down. She thought it might be cold so she drew a blanket around her, a blanket she had knotted and tied. Honey would fill her dreams. Aage had never felt so warm or comfortable, it was time to rest. Aage closed her eyes while the candles, silently burned themselves out.

Ioman woke Searlait when he got home. "Let's go for a walk, the night is beautiful, the stars are bright."

"It is so late, where have you been?"

"I was with Levian, come we'll bring a blanket and lay in the grass. You can tell me about the stars."

"I have told you about the stars, you never remember." He took her hand and led her to the meadow. "It's not that I don't remember, I like to hear your voice, you have a beautiful voice."

"I see, you want something, talking so sweet."

"I do I want you to come lay on this blanket with me and love me, wife,"

"That I can do husband." Searlait smiled a coy smile. Ioman spread the blanket out and helped her to the ground. He sat behind her, so she could lean back against his chest.

"You have been with Levian this whole night, what have you been doing?"

"Levian is a young man, he feels restless. There is nothing for him on the island."

"I suppose that is true, I hadn't thought of that."

"Well, I am his Papa, a young man needs to talk things over with his Papa." Ioman rocked her gently back and forth, he kissed her cheek, and neck, snuggled her ear and breathed a sigh of contentment.

"Is there a solution to his problem?"

"Hum, yes, you may not like it, but it will be all right."

"Tell me, your keeping me waiting."

"All right wife, Mamer. We talked with a captain, his name is Joesph France, he has a merchant ship, he buys our honey, Levian acquired passage to work on his ship."

"When does this happen?"

"Tomorrow, he will come and see you before he leaves , it will be after the festival."

"What about this Captain, do you trust him? What does he look like? Is this boat sound?"

"Right now he is stopping me from making love to the most beautiful wife." He started to kiss her neck again, covered her shoulder in warm lips, he blew warm air in her ear.

"Husband, please tell me, this is our boy I want to know."

"Yes wife. He is a fair minded man, very strict. He is tall, not taller then me." Ioman smiled. "He is a dark man, along in his years, he hopes to retire soon. The Ship, not a boat, is very beautiful, and well maintained."

"You saw it then, did you meet the crew?"

"Did you think I would just let him go on any rundown boat? I did meet some of the crew, they seemed very happy. The Captain doesn't tolerate disrespect or anger. Levian will be fine, he will learn much, and I'm sure he will be back from time to time. He couldn't leave his Mamer for long. Is that better?"

"If you think it is all right, I suppose I will have to be." She sighed a mother's sigh of worry.

"Now woman, tell me about the stars."

"I don't want to."

"You just want to worry? Worry is a waste of time. I am not worried. Do you not trust my judgment?" Ioman softly moved her chin upward so she could see his eyes. He kissed her gently. She smiled a sad little smile.

"He has grown up." She conceded. "Do you ever think about the Azure? What happened to your people? There are so many questions about what we left behind. Do you regret leaving? Levian might regret leaving."

"Regret? No. I wanted a life with you. That could not happen there. I'm happy with our odd little family, no war, no strife, our Bibi," Ioman smiled. "Life has been easy here, really, work, but I like work. The Azure were in decline, the women unhappy, the men unhappy. Only you and I had a future is what I think. The Azure would have to find their own way, if there was a way to be found."

He drew the veil back from her chest and said, "now tell me about these stars." He ran his hand over her breast, "where is my star?" He lingered at a soft nipple. "Or is it here with this one," her reached between her legs "or here?" She giggled. "Oh I think I found it, it is here," his fingers traced her lips. "Really, tell me about these stars." He traced the tattoo on her chest. "Do I have a star in here? I have to have a star, how can we spend all of eternity together if I don't."

"It is there!" Searlait was leaning back looking into the sky. She pointed and sat up, "Ioman, there are my stars! I have never been able to find them. What do you think it means?" The mother of the sun star pattern gleamed from the blue blackness. Searlait started to hum the welcome song. Ioman was quiet. He wrapped his arms around her. They stood, both transfixed by the night sky. A warm breeze swirled around them. Searlait's veils caught the breeze and drew Ioman closer to her. Small stars fell through the darkness with blue streaks of light, raining above their heads. Suddenly the breeze shifted, dark cool fingers crept around them, they seemed to leave the ground, star dust sparkled in a milky cloud that enveloped them, Ioman whispered "I love you." In a moment they we're stolen away. Together they joined The Gens D'Etoile stars in the cool hollows that had waited for them. Years later, when their stars were discovered, by men not yet dreamed of, they were called the Veiled Lovers. They were two stars that looked like one, locked in a fluttering blue cloud, embracing one another for eternity.

The Festival of the Sun

Levian was at the shore that morning. He woke up on the sand, wearing only the thin linen pants of the festival season. He groaned in pain, his head throbbed with the night's drink. As he sat up he could smell himself, again he groaned in displeasure. The sea lapped in gentle enticing undulations. He submerged himself in the sea, it's refreshing power momentarily got his legs to carry him out onto the road. The tavern was closed, the road vacant, Levian's throat was dry as a crumpled paper. The Sun was cresting the horizon, the festival would be started. Levian could find water there, he started the march towards the town center when his knees collapsed, he fell forward on his face. His eyes closed and he lay in the road. The day wove around him, it was patient for his arrival. The way the heart awaits love.

A child woke him with a poke on the end of his nose. She was dressed as a sunflower. "Levian, you are missing the festival. You've missed the Sun Greeting. And you are covered in dust." She said as a matter of fact. Levian sat up and stood, with a wobble. The child was gone before he could thank her. He could hear the festival, like a heart beat. The child was right, he was covered with the golden dust that blanketed the island, it sparkled with mineral. Only the poke he had received on the end of his nose showed his true color. His morning bath a distant memory. His throat still cried for water, he made his way to the festival. A cloud of dust swirling behind him, his very steps seemed to shake the ground.

The people of Gobelin took weeks to plan the festival. They made costumes, decorations adorned every doorway, images of the sun abound. There were sun kites, paper lanterns, and garlands of flowers hung from every post and wall. The smells of roasting meat, and baked sweets swam through the air. The crowd was dancing, chanting, laughing, they clapped linen pouches filled with powdered chalk, yellow, blue, red and green. It filled the air. To Levian it all appeared dreamlike. As he walked into the crowd he was met with an explosion of cheers, they were calling him the Sun King, someone put a makeshift crown on his head and draped a cape around his shoulders. He could barely decipher their words or faces. He made it to the well in the center of the square and drew himself a bucket of water. He put it to his lips and drank, and drank. When the bucket was half empty he poured the rest over his head, knocking his crown to the ground, someone promptly replaced it, and the cheering continued. Levian lowered himself into a chair, that had been brought for him. He held tightly onto the bucket. His head slumped onto his chest his eyes closed and the festival spiraled around him.

When Levian opened his eyes it was to an eerie fog. The crown was gone, the cape was gone, the bucket, the chair, the crowd. The square was empty, the fog was almost impenetrable, he got to his feet. He was disoriented, the sun was barely visible high above the fog. Below him a fog horn blew three sharp blows. Levian strained to make out the wharf. He headed towards the sound. He walked a few yards and fell off an embankment. He flipped over on himself several times before coming to a stop on a wooden walkway, " that's one way," he said to himself. It may as well have been the dead of night. Three more sharp blows of the fog horn blew. He must be on the wharf, the horn was close. He heard a voice, muffled by the fog, but it could lead him, and he walked towards it, ignoring the pain from the fall, he must have broken his arm. "HEY, HEY." He yelled. A voice answered him shouting "THIS WAY, HURRY, THIS WAY! The fog horn blew three more blasts, Levian ran towards the voice. He tried to quell the panic in his head. More voices joined in to lead the way. Suddenly in front of him were two men with lanterns at the end of a gangplank. "NOW, HURRY." They yelled. They ran up the plank together. Levian was on a ship. One man took him by the arm, "STAY HERE ." He yelled, pushing him against a rail. "ALL ABOARD." He yelled . Other men shouted. "LIFT THE GANGPLANK." "BRING UP THE ANCHOR."

Levian heard the chain of the anchor, footsteps ran just feet in front of him. Panic seemed to have taken over, he stood where he had been placed, hoping he was not in the way. He felt the ship jolt, the fog horn blew, the ship strained to move, the air was still and thick. "HOIST THE MAIN SAIL." Was shouted from the upper deck. Men had been staged with poles to push them out to sea. "CAST THE

LINE." Soon they had moved out of the harbor and the waves took them in hand. Orders were being shouted, "HOIST THE FORE SAILS. TIGHTEN THE MISSEN." Soon the lanterns glowed to life and allowed the deck to be seen. Levian was on board The Marchand. A collective calm came over the deck crew as they got further from the island. The fog lifted and the sun was high above them. The lanterns were extinguished. Levian stood at the end of the boat looking back at Gobelin. It was engulfed in a fog that seemed to come from the heavens. He wondered if he would ever see it again, and was half afraid of the answer his heart told him. As the island drifted out of sight, the voices around him seemed to lift in spirit, warmed by the sun. The panic felt only moments ago felt like a childhood fear now waved off. Gobelin was forgotten as the sails filled with wind. A cheer from the crew brought an energy filled joy that took over the ship, adventures waited for them all.

CPSIA information can be obtained
at www.ICGtesting.com
Printed in the USA
LVHW042309180723
752480LV00005B/988

9 781977 261663